Anna Banana

Nancy Gorrell

CHRISTIAN FOCUS

© Copyright 2006 Nancy Gorrell
ISBN 978-1-84550-182-2
Published in 2006 by
Christian Focus Publications,
Geanies House, Fearn, Tain
Ross-shire, IV20 1TW,
Great Britain
Cover design by Catherine Mackenzie
Cover illustration and inside illustrations
by Kim Spongaugle
Printed and Bound in Denmark
by Nørhaven Paperback A/S

Contents:

Who is Anna?

Who is Anna Banana and where does she live? Well, Anna Banana is just a nick name - one that Corey Redmond has given her - pesky boy! Anna's real name is Anna Freeling and she lives in a town in America with her

family. Anna's dad works in the local church, her mom makes really great

blueberry muffins, and her little brother D.J. is crazy about dinosaurs. Anna loves pretty things, and is a little bit scared of the dark ... not a lot ... just a little bit.

Anna has lots of friends, and one of her best friends is Jessica. Jessica has long blonde hair and blue eyes and lives only a few streets away.

Corey doesn't live too far away either... But Corey Redmond is one of those boys who gets into trouble even when he isn't trying. And he's just about to get into trouble with Anna...

Anna Banana

'Anna Banana!! Anna Banana!!'

Anna frowned. Corey knew she hated that nickname.

'Why does Corey always call me that?' Anna glared at the boy.

'Whatcha' doing, Anna Banana?'

'Waiting for my mom.'

Five-year-old Anna stared down at her hands.

Her mom had asked her to wait for just a few minutes outside the church library. Anna and her dolly Rose had been sitting patiently for what was beginning to seem a terribly long time.

'I see you have your ugly Posey Nosey Rosey doll with you!' Corey teased.

'She's not ugly!' Anna said quietly, but she felt tears coming into her eyes. She wished Corey would go away. Where was her mom?

'Hah! Let me see if she is'—and to Anna's horror, Corey grabbed Rose from the bench! 'Yes, she sure is!' He jeered as he swung the doll around by her hair. 'Ugly Ugly Ugly!'

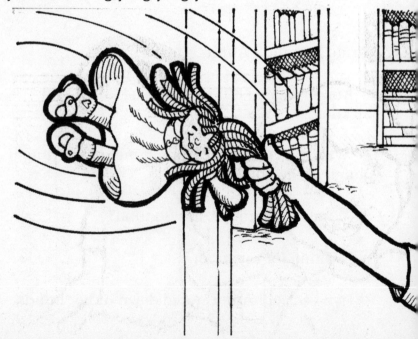

'Stop!' said Anna, trying not to yell.

'What a stupid, ugly dolly!' Corey continued and now held Anna's precious doll above her head beyond her reach. Anna was starting to panic.

Suddenly, in a fit of meanness, Corey threw Rose to the floor. Pushing Anna back, he stepped on Rose's smiling face with his horrible dirty boy boot!

Anna couldn't help crying now and yelling too! 'Stop it!' and she pulled at Rose with all her might.

Rose was freed, but a handful of her beautiful black hair was lying on the floor, and Rose's happy pink cheek had a dreadful brown heel mark on it.

'She looks better now!' Corey exclaimed at the half-bald and muddy doll. He took the black yarn hair and threw it into the air with glee. 'Ugly Nosey Rosey! Anna Banana!'

Right at that very same moment both Anna's mom, Mrs. Freeling, and Corey's mom, Mrs. Redmond, appeared in the hallway.

'Anna, child, why are you yelling—?' said Mrs. Freeling, but almost as soon as she asked, she saw Rose. Anna threw herself into her mother's arms.

Mrs. Redmond's face became quite red as she took her son by the shoulder. 'Corey, stop it!'

Corey did stop, but not very willingly. His eyebrows lowered, and he turned his face away from Anna and her mother. Poor Mrs. Redmond didn't know what to do, 'Anna, I'm so sorry,' she said. But Anna just pressed her face harder against her mom's neck and sobbed.

Mom let Anna ride in the
front on the way home.
She buckled Rose into the
seat between them, but
Anna didn't want to
look at her doll. The
dirty black heel mark
made her want to
cry again.

'Anna, I'm
sorry. Maybe we can clean her face.' Anna just
looked out the window and sniffled.

Daddy and Anna's little brother D.J. were
playing in the yard when Anna and her mother
pulled into the driveway.

'Hi, honey! Did you find the book?' Dad said to
Mom as they got out of the car. 'Hi, sweetie!' he
said to Anna.

Anna's tears started down her pale face, and
Rose hung limply in her arms.

'What happened?' Dad said, looking to Mom.

'Corey Redmond,' Mom whispered back.

'Oh, honey,' said Daddy gently, and he scooped
up Anna and Rose and carried them into the
house.

Anna and Dad sat together in the rocker until dinner time.

D.J. left the two of them on their own as he looked at his dinosaur books and roared at Mommy in the kitchen.

'Dinner's ready!' Mom called. Dad carried Anna to her seat. D.J. clambered into his high chair, and everyone was ready for prayer.

'Anna,' said her mother kindly, 'Why don't you pray tonight? You could ask the Lord Jesus for help. You could pray for Corey and his family too.'

Anna scowled. 'I don't want to pray,' she said grumpily. 'I don't want to eat, and I'm angry at Corey!'

'Anna,' her father spoke carefully, 'It's not wrong to be sad about Rose, but it's not right to be disobedient or ungrateful. I would like to read you something special after dinner.'

So Daddy thanked God for the food. Anna didn't talk much during supper that night.

After the meal, Dad opened his Bible. Anna's family always did this after every evening meal.

It was a special family time. It was time to think about God and to tell him that they loved him. Anna's family called this time 'Family Devotions.'

It was a special time of the day, and Anna looked forward to it. She climbed onto her dad's lap and snuggled down. D.J. sat with Mom. They listened quietly to Dad as he read some verses from the Bible.

That evening he turned to a book in the Bible called The Book of Romans.

'I'm reading from Romans chapter 8 verses 28-29,' Dad told them.

'We know that in all things

God works for the good of those

who love him, who have been called

according to his purpose.

For those God foreknew,

he also predestined to be conformed

to the likeness of his Son.'

Anna wondered what those words really meant.

'Anna,' Daddy said, 'Did you know that if you are God's child, everything that happens to you is for your good? Even bad things! God has a reason for it, and that reason is to make you more like Jesus. Tell me, Anna, were people ever unkind to Jesus?'

Anna nodded. She remembered the stories in the Bible.

Sometimes people had made fun of Jesus. Sometimes they had hurt him.

'Jesus was killed by people who hated him,' Anna told her father.

'And what did he say about how we should treat those who are unkind to us?'

'Be nice?' Anna said reluctantly.

'Yes, and more than that, ' Daddy said. 'Listen

to what Jesus said about how we should treat our enemies—those who are cruel to us and may even hate us:

> But I tell you: Love your enemies,
>
> and pray for those who persecute you,
>
> that you may be sons of your Father in heaven.
>
> He causes His sun to rise on the evil
>
> and the good, and sends rain on
>
> the righteous and the unrighteous.
>
> (Matthew 5:44-45)

'Anna, if someone hurts you or hates you, do you want to be kind to them or give them gifts?'

'No!'

'But that's just what God does! He sends rain and sunshine and other blessings to bad people. He also sent his very best gift to people who hated him. All of us have sinful hearts that run away from God and disobey him.

But God sent his Son Jesus to people who were his enemies.

Everyone who doesn't love Jesus is his enemy. But it is God who changes their hearts and makes them his friends instead of his enemies!

'Think of the wonderful thing that God did for you, Anna. He sent Jesus, his only son, to save you. He did this because he loves you. You can go to heaven to be with Jesus because he died on the cross to save you from sin. God gave you the gift of his Son and his forgiveness. He can help you to be kind to Corey now and to forgive Corey as he has forgiven you. God can use this circumstance to make you more like his Son.

'Anna, every time you look at that boot mark on Rose's face or that bald spot on her head,

instead of being sad or angry at Corey, why don't you say a prayer for the Redmond family instead?'

Anna squirmed a little in her seat, but she listened quietly.

'Now, what should you do to Corey? God tells us how to treat those who are unkind to us:

> Do not repay anyone evil for evil...
>
> If your enemy is hungry, feed him;
>
> If he is thirsty, give him something to drink...
>
> Do not be overcome by evil, but overcome evil with good. (Romans 12:17-21)

'Anna, tomorrow you will see Corey in Sunday School. How can you obey God's word here? Can you think of a kind thing to do for him?'

Anna thought carefully over the verses that she had just heard and finally said, 'Give him something good to eat?'

Mom laughed. 'OK, Anna, why don't we make blueberry muffins for Sunday School snack tomorrow?'

Anna's face brightened. Mommy's blueberry muffins were yummy!

'And,' Mom added, 'Let's make an extra special one just for Corey.'

Anna wasn't as happy about that, but she remembered the verses and she agreed.
'OK, Mommy. Can I stir in the blueberries?'

'Sure, sweetie.'

So they made delicious blueberry muffins that night.

The best muffin of all was an extra-large, extra-tasty muffin—a special muffin just for Corey.

Anna Banana

The next morning at
snack time, Mrs. Wheeler
said to the class, 'Anna
brought a very nice treat
today. She and her mom
made blueberry muffins
for us! Anna, would you
pass them out, please?'

Anna gulped and
picked up the muffin
container. She opened it and
went straight to the spot at the
table where Corey was sitting alone.
Corey fidgeted and didn't look up at her. Then, to
his surprise (and Anna's as well!), Anna reached
for the beautiful prize muffin and laid it on
Corey's napkin.

Corey's eyes widened. 'Thanks, Anna Ba—' but
he stopped! He didn't say it. He didn't say Anna
Banana!

Anna's eyes widened too. 'You're welcome,' she
said. And then she smiled. She smiled at Corey!

Anna had a funny light feeling on the inside
when Sunday School was finished. All the
children trooped up the stairs to the big hall
where the adults were waiting. Anna's father was
preaching today. Everybody sat down together to
listen to the lesson.

Anna sat down in the church with D.J. and her mom. She watched Corey closely as he walked up the aisle. He sat with his mother and a man Anna didn't recognize.

The man seemed uncomfortable in the wooden pew. He sat still and straight and kept his hand on Corey's shoulder the whole time. Needless to say, Corey didn't move an inch that morning.

Anna tried very hard to listen to her father during the sermon. He was talking about how God loved the world so much that he'd sent Jesus to die on the cross. Anna knew that Jesus had died on the cross so that all the people who trusted in him could be saved and go to heaven when they

died. Anna's dad said that if you trusted in Jesus you were born again; it was just like having a brand new life.

Anna's eyes strayed over to Corey again. He certainly had been sitting very, very still. He hadn't even itched his nose!

After church, she saw Corey and his mom go over to talk with her father, and the strange man went too.

Anna's Dad and the other man shook hands, and after a short time, both were smiling. Corey just stood quietly.

Then Anna's dad shook hands again, and waved goodbye.

Dad was cheerful on the way home. He looked over at Mom.

'That was Corey's dad!' he exclaimed. 'I guess he came because he felt that Corey needed a little extra supervision. I think he was embarrassed about what his son did to our little girl! What do you think, Anna? Because of Rose, Mr. Redmond came to church today. And what a good day to come! We should thank God.'

Anna wondered for a moment why it was such a good day for Corey's dad to come and then she realised... Corey's dad had heard that Jesus loved him and that Jesus wanted to forgive his sins.

Anna remembered what her father had said about good things and bad things. God can let bad things happen for our good.

'I guess it was good that Corey's dad came to church today ... even though Rose got all mussed up !'

But it was still hard for Anna to think about her doll, all scuffed and messy. Poor Rose!

For the next few days, Anna left Rose in her rocking chair in the bedroom. It was hard to see her dirty face and her missing hair.

Anna tried to pray for Corey and his family as Daddy had suggested. That wasn't easy to do but it helped to make the angry feeling inside go away. And, as the days passed, it was easier for Anna to be distracted. She had a birthday coming up and a party to plan!

First, Anna picked the games for the party. Then Mom took her and D.J. to the store and let Anna choose the napkins and plates.

Anna picked plates with pink flowers for the girls, and she picked others with green dinosaurs for the boys, because D.J. liked them best.

The girls got pink candy hearts for their cupcakes, and D.J. found candy dinosaurs for the boys.

Mom bought green and pink streamers. Anna could hardly wait for Saturday!

'Mom, did you send the invitations?' Anna asked eagerly when they were home again.

'Yes, Anna, to all the children in your Sunday School class, just as you asked.'

Anna had a sudden fearful feeling. 'But not to Corey!' she whined.

'Now, Anna, we decided to invite the whole class this year, and Corey is in it.'

'Yes, but we said that before Corey started coming to church!'

'Sweetie, I thought that you had been praying for Corey.'

'Yes, Mom, but he's still not my friend!'

'Anna, how many friends does Corey have at church?'

Anna thought for a moment.

'None, I guess.'

'Remember what the Bible said about being kind to others? Maybe Corey could make some friends here at the party! Wouldn't that be a wonderful thing? Besides, how would you feel if everyone but you was invited to a party?'

'I would be sad. I guess it's OK.'

But Anna just wasn't sure.

On Friday night Anna went to the rocking chair to get Rose and take her down to see the decorations. But Rose wasn't to be found.

'Mom, where's Rose? D.J., did you take her?'

'No,' said D.J. from his room.

'Anna, now don't blame your brother. I know that Rose will turn up soon. Come down and help me finish putting the candies on these cupcakes.'

'Yes, Mom,' Anna said and slowly came downstairs. The sprinkles were a lot of fun. Mom would probably help her find Rose in the morning.

Saturday morning dawned cheerful and sunny. Anna and D.J. rushed through breakfast, and then Anna skipped upstairs to put on her pink

party dress. Too bad she didn't have a pink dress for Rose. Only a torn yellow one. But wait! Still no Rose to be found!

Anna looked under the bed and inside the toybox again. She really wanted Rose at the party. She didn't mind so much now about the ugly heel mark. Where could she be?

Anna started to call for Mom and then the doorbell rang. Oh, how could she have a party without Rose?

The voices in the hallway made her peek out of her room.

'Is someone here for the party already?' she wondered.

Corey and Corey's mom were standing in the hallway.

'It was very kind of you to offer to help.' Mom was saying to Mrs. Redmond. 'These parties can be a lot of work.'

Dad had come out to shake her hand. 'Yes, thanks very much indeed. You ladies call me when you need me.'

Dad then laughed and retreated with his book.

'Anna!' Mom called. 'Please come down—Corey is here!'

Anna was almost glad that she hadn't found Rose. Rose was probably safer wherever she was for now.

She came reluctantly down the stairs. 'Hi, Corey.'

'Hi, Anna.' Corey mumbled. His face was really red, Anna noticed. Her mother and Mrs. Redmond walked a few steps away.

Corey looked at his mom and then down at the floor.

'Anna, I want to tell you that I'm very sorry about what I did to Rose.'

To Anna's surprise, he looked as if he might cry.

Corey stuttered and then said, 'Will you please forgive me?'

Anna didn't know what to say. Corey seemed very much as though he meant what he said. Anna's eyes filled with tears too. 'OK,' she said simply, 'I forgive you.' And she meant it as well.

'Oh,' said Corey in a relieved rush, 'and I have a present for you too!' He held out a very pretty package with a large pink bow.

'Thank you!' Anna said as she took the box from his outstretched hands and touched the bright pink bow admiringly.

'Open it!'

'Now?' Anna asked. 'Mommy, may I?'

'Just this one,' Mom responded, smiling.

'Hooray! Come on!'
and she and Corey ran
to the family room
and plopped down on
the floor.

Off came the shiny
pink bow and the
flowery wrapping paper.
Off came the lid. More
tissue paper. Anna pulled
it out quickly.

And what to her amazed
eyes should appear there in the
depths of the box?

Rose! Rose?

But she was fixed and
more beautiful than ever.
The dirty heel mark was
gone. The lovely thick black
hair was as perfect as the
day she was new.

And wonder of wonders, Rose was dressed in
the most charming pink party dress Anna had
ever seen!

'Oh, Rose,' Anna breathed. 'You look beautiful!'

And there was more!

Underneath Rose were more pretty doll dresses. A yellow one with checks, a white one with brightly colored polka dots, and a purple one with tiny violets!

'Do you like them?' Corey asked shyly.

'Oh, yes!' Anna picked up Rose and danced. 'Oh, yes! Thank you so much!'

'I think you should thank Mrs. Redmond as well,' Mommy laughed. 'She made all those lovely things for Rose.'

'Oh, thank you, Mrs. Redmond!'

'You're very welcome, Anna,' Mrs. Redmond responded, beaming as Anna waltzed around her, spinning Rose. Corey watched happily.

'Anna,' said Mom, 'If you can stop dancing, why don't you and Corey come and help us put out the party things?'

'OK, Mom,' Anna said and pulled Corey into the dining room. 'Here, Corey, you put the dinosaur plates out for the boys.'

Anna Banana

'Sure thing, Anna Banana,' said Corey, and he smiled at her.

Anna smiled back. She decided she really didn't mind that nickname after all.

ASK ABOUT IT

 What was Anna's problem? Who was annoying her?

 What does Anna's Dad do at church?

 What kind of muffin did Anna make with her mom?

 Who got the biggest and the best muffin?

Anna Banana

God tells us to forgive our enemies and those who persecute us. Someone who is a "persecutor" may call you names, hurt your feelings, or even bully you. Some Christians have persecutors who have harmed their bodies or even killed them. Jesus had persecutors who put him to death on the cross. Think of the love that Jesus showed to those bad people! While he was dying there, he asked God to forgive his enemies. Did you know that before God makes you his own, you are his enemy too? God showed amazing love by sending his own Son to die for sinners. If you are a Christian, God has changed your heart, and he can make you willing and able to love your enemies as well. If someone is hurting and bullying, you tell a grown-up and ask for help. You should also tell your Saviour, Jesus. He is the One who can help you love and forgive.

WHAT WOULD YOU DO?

 If someone was mean to you and bullied you - what would you do? Pick your answers.

 Be just as mean to them.

Be even nastier to them.

Tell a parent, or grown-up.

Be kind to them.

Forgive them.

Pray for them.

WHAT DID ANNA DO?

Anna told her parents about what was happening. It is important to tell a grown-up if someone harms you. Anna wanted to be unkind to Corey in return but her parents taught her that this was wrong. Anna prayed for Corey, but even then it was hard to be nice to him. Even though Anna did give Corey the best blueberry muffin, she still didn't want him to come to the party. But in the end she forgave him. God helped her to forgive Corey and to do what Jesus wanted her to do.

Fright in the Night

Out of the corner of her eye, Anna thought she saw a movement in her closet. She looked again. Hadn't she closed that door? What was that rustling sound? Anna's shoulders stiffened.

'Raaaaaaaruh!'

Anna shrieked. 'Mom!!'

'Raaaroooraaa! Bwahaha! T Rex will eat you!' D.J. roared.

'Momeee! Mom! D.J. stop it, you meanie! You scared me!'

'Ha, ha! Boo!'

'Mom!' embarrassed and angered by D.J.'s laughter, Anna pulled the covers over her head.

A silly D.J. was bouncing around the room, roaring thunderously.

'Please make him be quiet!' She couldn't believe she hadn't heard him sneak out of bed. 'Why was he able to scare me so badly?' she groaned inside.

'D.J.' came a stern voice from the doorway. It wasn't Mom, but Anna's father. 'Why are you out of bed? Come here, young man!'

At the sound of Dad's command, D.J. was immediately silent and Went There. And so off they two went, as they often did. And back they came again, D.J. repentant, as usual. 'Sorry, Anna. Please forgive me.'

'I forgive you.' Anna gave him a hug. 'Goodnight, D.J. I love you.'

'I love you, too.'

Fright in the Night

In the dark once more, D.J. tucked snugly in the bed across from her, a tired but an apprehensive Anna glanced over at the closet again.

She heard her brother wiggle and then fall into peaceful, steady breathing. Anna pulled the blanket back over her head and finally went to sleep.

Surprised, Anna realised that she was actually standing beside the front door of her house. 'How did I get here?' she wondered. Gingerly she opened the door and squinted into the bright sunlight. Anna stepped out, closed the door behind her, and looked into the yard. For some reason, Rose was lying on the grass, so she walked over to pick her up.

Halfway back across the lawn, Anna suddenly heard a growl from behind one of the bushes. Her heart started pounding as she saw a strange dog, teeth bared, move from the shadows and look straight at her. The dog growled again, a rumbling deep in its throat, and started to race towards her.

Clutching Rose, Anna ran to the door, but it wasn't her house! Despite that fact, she grasped the doorknob frantically. It was locked!

'Help! Help!' she cried and tried to run, but her legs just wouldn't move. They felt so stiff and heavy. She knew the dog was getting closer...

'Help!' she called again.

'Anna, what is it?' came a welcome voice and a hand on her arm. 'Anna, it's OK. Wake up, sweetie, it's only a dream.' Anna struggled to open her eyes.

Fright in the Night

'Oh, Mom, it was a terrible dream.' Warm arms were around the frightened little girl, and her mother's soft cheek was pressed against her hair. Anna felt a rush of relief to be awake and in her bedroom, not outside with a vicious, angry dog. She snuggled close to her mother's comforting presence.

'What...' came a mumble from the next bed.

'It's OK, D.J., go back to sleep,' said Mom. D.J. groaned and turned over, obediently snoring.

Anna rested peacefully in her mother's arms for a while. It was just a dream. Everything was

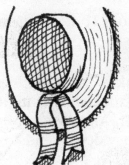 

Anna

fine... She felt a gentle kiss on her forehead as she relaxed into slumber.

'Good thing it's Saturday,' Anna's mother smiled over a cup of coffee as a tangly-haired Anna dragged herself into the kitchen the next morning.

'I didn't sleep so well,' Anna wilted into a chair.

'I know, honey, I was up too! That's your second nightmare in just a few days.'

'Dinosaurs, dogs, and snakes,' Anna replied, drooping. But the smell of pancakes was inviting, and a little maple syrup later, Anna was quite perky and ready to face a busy day, the last night forgotten.

By the time evening rolled around, Anna was tired, but once again, the thought of bedtime put a knot in her stomach.

'Mom, may I sleep in your room tonight? I'll put a sleeping bag on the floor. Please?'

'Me too, me too,' D.J. chimed in. 'Let's camp in Mom and Dad's room! We can make popcorn! We could wrestle with Dad!'

'Now, children,' was the answer, 'You know your father has to be rested tomorrow. I don't think camping in our room is such a good idea.'

'Please?' Anna pouted.

'Not tonight, Anna. Now it's time for both of you to go to bed! Brush your teeth, please, and put on your pyjamas, and then we'll pray. And we'll definitely ask for no nightmares tonight, won't we?'

Anna felt a little better. 'Definitely.'

No bad dreams for several days left Anna less uncomfortable about bedtime. It was just too bad when Bobby from two doors down stopped by late one afternoon, as Anna was picking up her toys from the yard.

Leaning over the fence, a gleam in his eye,
Bobby told Anna that there was a hungry tiger,
escaped from the zoo, hiding in the neighborhood
and looking for a victim. Anna knew that Bobby
was a rotten tease, who loved to scare her; but she
was terrified anyway and ran inside crying to her
mother.

Bobby, of course, disappeared quite quickly.

Nothing her mother could say made her ready
for bed that evening!

'But he strikes at night, Mom! Bobby said so!
He's looking for a victim!'

Fright in the Night

Dad dropped his book onto his lap. 'Who strikes at night? What's going on? And who's this Bobby that's been telling my Anna stories?'

Thankfully, D.J. was already tucked in and slumbering as Anna repeated Bobby's unkind tale. Dad stared thoughtfully at the wall, frowning.

'Anna,' he finally asked, 'Is my little girl afraid of the dark?'

'I don't know whether I'm afraid of the dark, Dad, but I'm definitely afraid in it.'

Anna's father laughed. 'I remember being afraid in the dark too, Anna. Do you know what helped me?'

'What?' Anna was curious.

'Psalms.'

'Psalms? The Book of Psalms?'

'Yes, Anna. Know what? I think sometimes even the brave warrior King David, who wrote many Psalms, was tempted to be afraid in the dark.'

'Really?' the thought surprised her.

'Sure. David wrote songs that speak about God's care in the day and in the night. They remind us that God never sleeps, h protects us, and his angels are all around us.

'Some of these Psalms were written at very difficult and dangerous times in David's life—and he had many true perils to concern him, not just pretend stories that unkind neighborhood boys made up.

'Anna, in the Psalms are verses that teach us how to handle our fear in the dark—verses that talk about praying, meditating, even singing in bed. Those are the things you should keep your mind busy with, when you are tempted to be afraid.'

'Singing in bed? That might be fun, but what about D.J.?'

'You can always have a song in your heart, Anna.' Dad smiled.

'Show me those verses, please.'

'How about a few tonight and more later on? You should choose some verses and whole Psalms to memorize too.'

'OK.'

So Anna and her father read several Psalms that evening. She chose Psalm 4 to memorize first and decided that she would read through the Psalms, one every night, before bedtime.

Anna read Psalm 4. 'The first verse and the last verse are my special verses for tonight,' Anna smiled to herself. She read the first verse out loud.

'Answer me when I call to you
O my righteous God.
Give me relief from my distress;

be merciful to me and hear my prayer.'

And then she read the last verse,

'I will lie down and sleep in peace,

for you alone, O Lord,

make me live in safety.'

When Anna's mother finally turned off the lights, it was still very dark. The shadows looked the same as always. Anna pulled her covers over her head and prayed.

Fright in the Night

She thought about some verses she already knew—Psalm 23. She knew a musical version of that one as well, so after she recited it in her head, she sang it in her heart.

Anna thought about sheep nibbling at the grass on the hillside and about the shepherd who looked after them. That was what the psalm meant when it said, 'The Lord is my shepherd.' It meant that God looks after his people just like a shepherd looks after his sheep.

Anna went through each verse of the song one after the other.

The Lord is my shepherd.

I shall not be in want.

He makes me to lie down in green pastures.

He leads me beside the still waters.

He restores my soul.

He guides me in paths of righteousness,

for his name's sake.

Even though I walk through

the valley of the shadow of death

I will fear no evil for you are with me.

Your rod and your staff they comfort me.

You prepare a table before me

in the presence of my enemies.

You anoint my head with oil.

My cup overflows.

Surely goodness and mercy

shall follow me all the days of my life

and I will live in the

house of God forever.

Singing in bed was fun, Anna decided.

Fright in the Night

After singing through it once, she started again, but that time she didn't even get to the third verse before she fell asleep.

As the days passed, Anna still struggled sometimes with worrying at night time.

Learning the Bible verses helped some.

Praying to God helped too, and the singing was great!

Before too long, the jumpy-stomach feeling at bed-time started to fade away.

Sleeping soundly one night, Anna was startled awake by a cry.

'Help! Help!'

It was D.J. Though it was dark, she could see him sitting up in bed and waving his arms. 'Stop! No!'

Anna jumped out of bed and ran to his side. 'What is it, D.J.? Wake up! It's only a nightmare. It's OK, really it is.'

D.J. was crying, but he was finally awake. 'I had a bad, bad dream. T Rex wanted to eat me!'

'Oh, D.J.!' Anna put her arms around her brother and laid her cheek against his hair. She didn't see her father move softly back from his rush to the door. 'It's OK, D.J. Jesus is with us, and he never sleeps. His angels are always watching over us.'

D.J. rested against her, listening quietly. He wiped his tears and hugged his sister. They sat in silence for a little while as he calmed back down.

'You know what helps me not to be afraid in bed, D.J.?' Anna said smiling.

'What?' he sniffled. 'Tell me.'

'Singing.'

'Singing in bed?'

'Sure, it's fun! I'll sing you Psalm 23.'

ASK ABOUT IT

 What did D.J. pretend to be when he scared Anna?

 What animal did Bobby tease Anna about?

 What two Psalms did Anna think about when she was worried?

 What did Anna do to help D.J. when he was frightened by his nightmare?

Fright in the Night

Do you sometimes feel worried and anxious about things? The Bible tells us that we should not worry about some things - like what clothes we are going to wear, or what food we are going to eat. God looks after us. He cares for us more than he cares for the sparrows, and he makes sure that they have food to eat. God cares for us more than he cares for flowers - and they look splendid.

When we do have things that trouble us we should ask God to help us. He is with us always. Jesus has promised that he will never leave us. Even in the night, even when we are far away from home, God is close to those who love him and trust in him.

Fright in the Night

WHAT WOULD YOU DO?

When you feel nervous and scared what should you do? Pick your answers.

⭐ Bite your nails.

⭐ Hide under the bed.

⭐ Run away.

⭐ Get help from a grown-up.

⭐ Sing a happy song.

⭐ Pray to God.

Fright in the Night

WHAT DID ANNA DO?

When D.J. roared, when it was dark and scary in her room, when Bobby told Anna about a fierce tiger ... Anna was scared. In her dreams she ran away. It is right to run away from danger - but dreams don't hurt you. Hiding or running doesn't help when it is a dream you are scared of. If you tell someone you are scared they might be able to help. Singing a happy song that reminds you of Jesus and God is a good idea. Speaking to God about your troubles - that's even better. Prayer helps. Jesus helps. We are safe with him.

Cool Jewel

'Anna, oh Anna, wait 'til I show you this!'

Anna's friend Jessica rushed into the Sunday School classroom and seated herself triumphantly next to Anna. She flipped her long, light hair back with a toss of her head.

'Look!'

'What? Where?' Anna asked excitedly.

'Oh, Anna,' Jessica sighed impatiently and wiggled her earlobe at Anna. 'Aren't they gorgeous?'

Anna's eyes
caught the sparkle
on her friend's ears.
She leaned closer.
Glittery blue stones
winked back at her.

'They're real,'
Jessica laughed and
touched the stones softly.
'Sapphires, Anna! Can
you believe it? My dad
gave them to me for my
birthday! He said I was his
precious blue-eyed girl.'

She batted long lashes at Anna.

'Sapphires? Really? Oh, Jessica, they're
wonderful…'

But Jessica was already up and away. 'Gracie,
look, look!'

A tittering gaggle of admiring girls began to
gather around Jessica's sparkling earlobes.

Anna stayed in her seat. She remembered
the last time she had been to Jessica Anderson's
home. She and Jessica had giggled their way
through Jessica's mom's jewelry catalogs.

Cool Jewel

'When I'm a grown-up, I'll get these ... and these .... and these ...' they had laughed and outdone each other trying to find the most outrageous jewelry in the magazines.

But as Anna looked at Jessica showing off the new jewelry she felt more than a little bit upset.

Anna did love pretty things and she didn't think it was fair that Jessica was allowed something that Anna could only dream about.

Anna actually felt jealous. Even though she was in Sunday school and should have been thinking about Jesus, Anna was thinking about jewelry the whole time.

All the way through the Bible reading, the singing and the story, Anna thought about the two little sapphires on Jessica's ears.

She didn't do any better during the church service, either. Anna daydreamed through the prayer and the teaching. All the time that she spent in church she was thinking about the pretty things that she really wanted ... especially Jessica's ear rings.

She tried to concentrate, but her mind kept straying away. Anna could think of nothing else but all the jewels she wanted to buy one day.

Anna's mother kept glancing over at her, so she pretended that she was listening to the Bible reading.

Anna looked towards the front and sang all the words, but she didn't think about what they meant. Instead of speaking to God during the prayer time Anna dreamed about diamonds and rubies.

When it was time to go home, Anna left church with a guilty feeling. 'I should have been listening,' she thought to herself, 'but I wasn't.' Anna sighed. She was glad that her mom didn't know where her mind had been that morning.

'Anna, what were you thinking about during church today?' her mother questioned on the way home.

Anna's cheeks flushed.

She wanted to lie and say 'Oh nothing.' But she felt rotten enough, and lying would just make it worse.

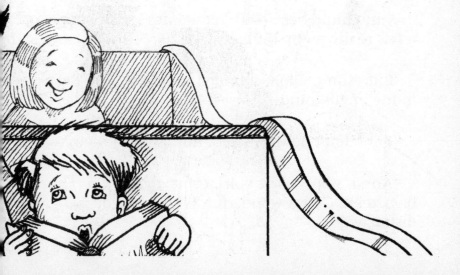

Dad's voice was kind as he drove the car along the freeway. 'Anna, God is wonderful. Why were you so distracted?'

Anna looked at the floor in shame.

'Going to church is a special time to think about Jesus. When we're in church it's a waste of time to think of anything else. If you've spent your time in church day-dreaming, Anna, then you've really missed out. What were you thinking about instead?'

Anna hung her head. 'Sometimes I wish I had a few really pretty things.'

'But, Anna,' Mom sounded surprised. 'You have many pretty things.'

'But I don't have any real things, like jewelry.'

'Anna, stop.' Dad's voice came again. 'Go back a bit. God is wonderful. Why were you so distracted?'

Then Dad asked Anna another question. 'Perhaps it has something to do with Jessica's new earrings?'

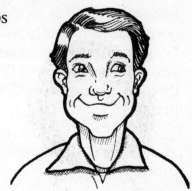

Anna was shocked. How could he know that?

'You ignored the one true God today, Anna. You spent your time thinking about trinkets. Are there idols in your heart? Are you coveting Jessica's earrings?'

Anna felt terribly ashamed and turned her head toward the window so D.J. wouldn't see her tears.

She remembered the Sunday school lesson about idols. An idol was anything that you loved more than the one true God. Sometimes statues and pictures were idols. Sometimes they were things that you owned or wanted to buy. Anna wondered if she actually loved earrings and jewelry more than she loved Jesus? She certainly had wished that Jessica's earrings were hers instead... and that was coveting. Anna knew that it was wrong.

'Anna,' Mom spoke gently, 'We have so many blessings in our lives and home. We have many good things to be thankful for. Be grateful for God's kindness to you and remember that he gives you all that you need. Be glad for Jessica, too, for the good things that God has given her in her life.'

'It is hard to be glad for Jessica —she was showing off!'

'Think kindly, Anna,' Dad said slowly, 'Think kindly of Jessica and be a friend to her. This afternoon I think you should spend some time with God. Ask him to forgive you. God can

change your heart and give you a love for the things that are really important. Earrings aren't precious - Jesus Christ is.'

Later that afternoon, as Anna sat alone in her bedroom, the phone rang. That wasn't unusual, but the noise and bustle that began immediately afterwards was very strange.

'What's going on?' Anna wondered as she listened to the anxious voices.

She heard her father as he spoke urgently into the phone. 'When? Where are they taking him? I'm on my way.'

There was a second or two of silence as the person on the other end of the phone continued to speak. And then Anna's dad exclaimed, 'Absolutely, we'll drive her to the hospital when you're ready.'

Anna wanted to listen some more, but her parents moved into the next room. Their voices became low and quiet and Anna couldn't hear them any longer.

Two minutes later Anna's father was backing down the driveway, and Anna's mom, with a concerned look, was closing the door behind him.

'Mom, what is it?' Anna pulled on her mother's arm.

'Anna, come here.'

She drew Anna over to the kitchen table so that they could both sit down.

'Mr. Anderson is very ill.'

'Jessica's dad?'

'Yes, Anna. We had hoped that it wouldn't get this bad, but apparently it has. Mr. Anderson will need surgery right away.'

'Surgery!' Anna's voice fell to a whisper. 'Is Mr. Anderson going to die?'

'Anna, we hope not, but he may be ill for a while. We need to pray for him and for his family too.'

'Poor Jessica.'

'Yes, indeed—poor Jessica, and Mrs. Anderson as well. Mr. Anderson's family is very precious to him. '

Anna's thoughts flew away. She remembered Jessica's words from this morning... 'My precious blue-eyed girl.'

Anna's mother continued talking, 'Jessica's on her way here, Anna. She is going to stay with us until her mother wants her at the hospital.'

She had barely finished her sentence when the doorbell rang. Anna jumped up anxiously.

'Now Anna,' warned her mother. 'Control yourself as best you can, so that you can be a help to Jessica. If you get all upset it will just make Jessica feel worse.'

Anna tried to smile as widely as she could. When her mother opened the door, a very small-looking, very pale Jessica stood on the doorstep. Anna's mother quickly gave Jessica a great big hug. The frightened little girl began crying in her arms. 'Will my Dad be all right?'

'I hope so Jessica. The doctors can help him and since we're worried, we should pray.'

And pray they did. Anna's mom spoke to Jesus about their troubles and asked him to look after Jessica's dad.

Anna listened to her mom's prayer and began to feel better - she hoped Jessica did too.

Slowly Jessica's tears began to dry.

As they opened their eyes to look at each other, Anna's mom smiled kindly at Jessica.

'You're shivering, Jessica. How about some hot chocolate, everyone?'

'Yes, please,'
Jessica smiled.

Anna reached for
Jessica's hand and
held it tightly as her
mom went to the stove.

The smell of the
chocolate soon filled
he air. D.J. immediately
appeared in the kitchen.

His first word was 'Yum!' and then, 'Jessica,
hooray!'

D.J.'s little arms shot up, and he wiggled a
dance step. Jessica smiled at him, a much bigger
smile than before.

D.J. became even sillier and started making
goofy noises. Everybody laughed and relaxed a
little.

Jessica thanked Anna's mom for the hot
chocolate. Her hands hugged a full, frothy, warm
mug with marshmallows sprinkled on the top.

As Jessica leaned over her mug, D.J. caught
sight of something shining on her ear.

'Oooh, pretty,' he said, leaning across the

table to touch, and, of course, spilling his cocoa everywhere.

'Oh, D.J.,' Mom sighed, smiling, as the girls giggled at his clumsiness. He 'helped' clean up and then tiptoed in front of Jessica.

'May I see?' he asked shyly.

Jessica pulled her silky blonde hair back so that D.J. could see the prized sapphire jewelry.

Gently, D.J. touched an earring and then looked into Jessica's face. 'Just like your eyes,' he said, sweetly and surprisingly observant. 'You look beautiful,' he whispered.

Jessica smiled tearfully and gave him a hug. 'Thank you, D.J.'

'They are beautiful,' said Anna. 'I'm so glad you got them.'

'I am too,' said Jessica, squeezing her earlobes tightly. 'My dad...' but she couldn't finish the sentence.

'They are a very special gift from your father,' said Anna's mom. 'I think he chose well.'

'So do I,' Jessica sighed deeply.

They sat around the table for a long while, talking quietly about whatever seemed to interest their visitor. When the dinner hour came, there were warm bowls of soup and fresh bread. The girls didn't feel very hungry, but Anna's mom insisted that everybody eat a proper meal.

When the phone finally rang, Jessica went white, staring at it fearfully.

Anna's mom was actually shaking a little herself as she answered the call.

'Yes. Yes.' A big breath escaped her. 'Oh, praise God.' She nodded at Jessica. 'Very good, we'll see you shortly. Goodbye.'

Anna saw that her mom was smiling. 'It must be good news,' she thought to herself.

Anna's mom sat down beside Jessica.

'The surgery went well. They've finished the operation, and your mother wants you to come

up to the hospital. It would be good if you were there so your dad can see you when he wakes up.'

Jessica looked relieved, happy, and nervous all at once. 'Can we go right now?'

'Yes, right now,' said Anna's mom. 'Anna, D.J., get ready. We need to leave.'

They scurried out to the car for a jittery ride to the hospital. Jessica and Anna clasped hands and fidgeted the whole way.

By the time they had come to the right floor, Jessica was almost shaking. At the first glimpse of her mother, she dropped Anna's hand and raced down the wide, white hallway. 'Mom! Is he still OK?'

Mrs. Anderson embraced her daughter. 'Yes, Jessica, Dad's fine. And they think he's already waking up!

They will be moving him to his own room very soon. Oh, thank God. Thank God!' She leaned on Anna's mom for support. 'Thank God.'

'Come on, you need to sit down.' Anna's mother opened the door to a waiting area. 'I'll go and tell a nurse where to find you, and then we can sit here for a while and talk.'

Mrs. Anderson sat down, weary, but smiling. When Anna's mom came back into the room Mrs. Anderson asked, 'Will you pray? I can hardly speak.'

'Certainly.' Anna's mom thanked God for the answer to their prayers and prayed that Mr. Anderson would recover quickly and completely.

Everyone said 'Amen,' and just then the door opened.

D.J. jumped out of his chair and ran up to the door for a closer look.

A kind-looking man, wearing a long white coat, stood in the doorway. His eyes circled the room until they fell on Jessica and Mrs. Anderson.

'Is there a beautiful lady and a blue-eyed girl in here?' he smiled. 'Someone's asking for them.'

Mrs. Anderson's eyes filled with tears of joy as she hugged Anna's mother goodbye.

Someone else stood in the hallway just behind the doctor.

Anna smiled when she recognised her dad. She clutched at her father as Jessica and her mom disappeared down the corridor.

'I love you, Daddy. I'm so glad Jessica's dad is all right.'

'Me too, honey. Me too.'

Anna's family slowly walked to the elevator together. Anna's father looked at his watch.

'I phoned the folks at church to tell them what had happened to Mr. Anderson. They've been having a special prayer meeting for him. I'm just so glad and thankful that I could give them some good news.'

He looked down at Anna. 'And I'm also glad and thankful that my Anna was a kind friend to Jessica this afternoon.'

They all stepped into the elevator together, and the doors closed quietly behind them.

'Anna,' said her father later that week, 'Let's go out for an ice cream.'

'Really?' Anna bounced up from her book. 'Now? Just us?'

'Yes, now, and yes, just us. How about it? Care to go out on a little date with me, young lady?'

'Certainly, sir,' Anna curtsied and whisked to the closet. 'I'll just get my coat!'

Anna loved the special times when Dad took her out. Sometimes they would laugh and be silly the whole trip. Other times, she would just hold his hand and go for walks. Ice cream was a favorite treat, so this was a particularly grand occasion.

Anna slurped all the way to the bottom of her ice cream float and sighed with pleasure.

Mr. Freeling chuckled. 'I always loved ice cream floats when I was young, too.'

Then he reached into his pocket, took out a dainty box and laid it on the table. 'I have a little present for you, Anna.'

Anna's eyes widened. 'Really? Yay! What is it?'

'Open it.'

'Yes, sir!' The small, unwrapped box was easily—and quickly—opened.

Inside was a tiny gold locket on a delicate chain. A little heart was finely etched on its surface.

Anna gasped. 'It's beautiful! Oh, Daddy, thank you!' She touched it
carefully and then suddenly
she looked up at her father,
a little concerned.
'Daddy, why...'

Mr. Freeling read
her eyes. 'Don't worry,
Anna,' he laughed.
'It's simply because
I love you. I bought
that locket for you a
year ago, but I was
waiting for the right
time to give it.'

'And now is the right time?'

'Yes, Anna. I was waiting for two things. First of all, I wanted to be sure that you were old enough to take care of something of value.'

'Oooh,' Anna breathed and touched the locket again.

'And,' her father added, 'most importantly, I wanted to be sure that my Anna had learned an valuable lesson.'

'What lesson is that?' Anna asked, surprised.

'Well, I wanted to make sure that you knew that all good things come from God. And I wanted to be sure that my Anna's heart would belong to the giver and not to the gift.'

Anna nodded thoughtfully. 'I think I understand,' she said.

'Let me show you something, Anna.' He took the locket and opened it. Inside the locket Anna saw her father's face smiling up at her.

'Anna, you can't begin to know how very much I love you.'

Anna gave a little squeal when she saw the wee picture of her father, then she darted around the table and threw her arms around his neck.

'Thank you, Daddy! I love you, too. Thank you for my beautiful necklace!'

'You're very welcome, my sweet girl. But although this gift is from your Daddy because he loves you ... all good gifts come from your Heavenly Father because he loves you ever so much. His love is much more valuable than gold.'

Anna wiggled gleefully. 'May I wear it?'

'Of course, your highness,' Anna's father laughed. 'Let me help you put it on.' He undid the clasp and reached around his daughter's neck to fasten it. 'There! It's beautiful. Just like you!'

Anna smiled and then gasped, 'Wait. Let me look at the picture again. It's so tiny! I love it! I love it because it's a picture of you!' She gave her dad another hug. 'Thank you, Daddy.'

Cool Jewel

That Sunday morning, Anna rushed into her classroom with a bright glint of gold sparkling around her neck. Her friend Jessica waved happily to her from the far corner, and Anna bounded in her direction.

'Jessica! Jessica! Wait 'til I show you this!'

ASK ABOUT IT

 What did Jessica get from her father?

 What colour were Jessica's eyes?

 Who had to go to hospital?

 Who really gives us all good things to enjoy?

Cool Jewel

Do you ever make a list of the things that you want? Perhaps you have a list of favorite foods or colours? God is the Creator of all things. He made the wonderful world we live in. He gives us all that we need - and more. God's love is truly amazing. He even gave his one and only Son, Jesus, whom he loved. Jesus died on the cross so that God's people could be forgiven for their sins. Trusting in Jesus for the forgiveness of our sins is the only way we can be with him, forever, in heaven when we die. This gift from God is something you cannot earn - gifts are given out of love. The gift of God is eternal life through Jesus Christ, our Lord.

Cool Jewel

WHAT WOULD YOU DO?

When you want something that belongs to someone else what should you do? Pick your answers.

 Take what you want when nobody is looking.

 Pester your parents until they give in and get you what you want.

 Sulk and complain because you never get 'nice' things.

 Save up for it.

 Pray to God for help to be happy with what you have.

 Thank God for all of his gifts.

Cool Jewel

WHAT DID ANNA DO?

Anna was jealous at first, wasn't she? She daydreamed her way through church - thinking more about the earrings than her wonderful God. Anna complained to her parents on the way home that she wished she had some nice things. Anna knew that this was wrong. She remembered how good God was to her. He had given her the most precious and beautiful gift. That gift was his Son Jesus Christ. Anna was thankful for Jesus and his love. She realised that God had given her lots of good things and that she should love God.

Nancy Gorrell

Nancy Gorrell takes great delight in telling about the Christian faith in simple ways for children to understand. She is married and lives with her husband and children in California.

Other Books by Nancy Gorrell:

Beginning With God
ISBN 1 85792 453 3
Living With God
ISBN 1 85792 532 7
Meeting With God
ISBN 1 85792 531 9

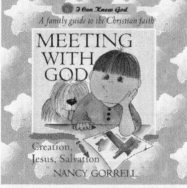

CHRISTIAN FOCUS PUBLICATIONS

Christian Focus **Christian Heritage** **CF4K** **Mentor**

Christian Focus Publications publishes books for adults and children under its three main imprints: Christian Focus, Mentor and Christian Heritage. Our books reflect that God's word is reliable and Jesus is the way to know him, and live for ever with him.

Our children's publication list includes a Sunday school curriculum that covers pre-school to early teens; puzzle and activity books. We also publish personal and family devotional titles, biographies and inspirational stories that children will love.

If you are looking for quality Bible teaching for children then we have an excellent range of Bible story and age specific theological books.

From pre-school to teenage fiction, we have it covered!

Find us at our web page:
www.christianfocus.com

CF4•K
Because you're never to young to know Jesus